D1572926

Rain & Hail

FRANKLYN M. BRANLEY
Illustrated by Harriett Barton

HarperCollins*Publishers*

Rain & Hail

The *Let's-Read-and-Find-Out Science Book* series was originated by Dr. Franklyn M. Branley, Astronomer Emeritus and former Chairman of the American Museum-Hayden Planetarium, and was formerly co-edited by him and Dr. Roma Gans, Professor Emeritus of Childhood Education, Teachers College, Columbia University. For a complete catalog of Let's-Read-and-Find-Out Science Books, write to HarperCollins Children's Books, 10 East 53rd Street, New York, NY 10022.

Rain & Hail

Rain comes from clouds.

It comes from big clouds and little clouds. It comes from black clouds and gray clouds.

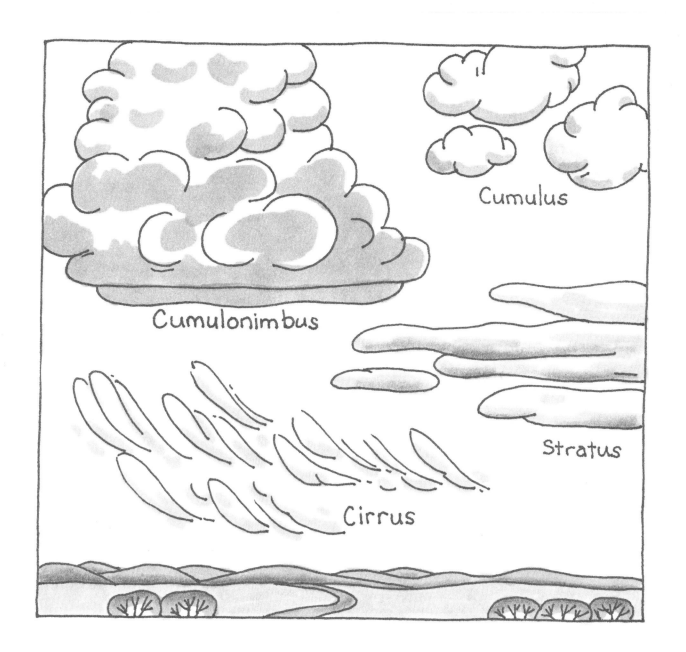

Cumulonimbus

Cumulus

Stratus

Cirrus

All clouds—big ones and little ones, gray clouds, black clouds and white ones—are made of billions of tiny drops of water. The drops are called droplets, because they are so small.

If this is the size of a drop of water, a droplet would be just a tiny speck, even smaller than this one.

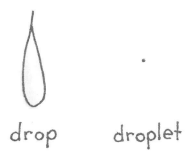

drop   droplet

Water droplets come from water vapor.

Water vapor is a gas. There is always water vapor in the air, but you cannot see it. You cannot smell it, and you cannot feel it.

Water vapor is made when water evaporates. That means the water changes from a liquid to a gas.

In the morning put a teaspoon of water in a saucer. That night it may all be gone. Heat in the room made it evaporate into the air.

When wet clothes hang on the clothesline, the water in them evaporates. The heat from the sun changes the water drops and droplets into water vapor. The water vapor goes into the air.

Most of the water vapor in the air
comes from lakes, rivers and oceans. It

comes from the leaves of plants, and from the wet ground.

The heat from the sun causes the water to evaporate. The water changes from a liquid to a gas. The water vapor goes into the air.

When you breathe out, you put water vapor into the air. Usually, you cannot see the water vapor. But it is there.

If it is cold, you can sometimes "see your breath." That's because the water vapor condenses. It changes from a gas to tiny droplets. Your breath makes a little cloud.

When cows and horses, dogs and cats, breathe out, they put water vapor into the air too. On a cold day, the droplets make little clouds that you can see.

You can make water vapor change to water. Put a lot of cracked ice into a glass

of water. As the glass gets colder, the
outside of the glass gets wet. Water vapor
in the air is condensing on the glass.
There may be so much that the glass drips.
Sometimes the glass stays dry. That means
there is not much water vapor in the air.

The air holds the water vapor. Breezes carry it from one place to another. Much of the vapor moves up and away from the earth.

Air above the earth is always cold. The higher you go, the colder it gets.

When air gets cold enough, the water vapor in it condenses. The vapor changes to water droplets.

The water droplets make clouds.

When clouds are thin and wispy, they are holding only a little water.

When clouds are thick and dark, they
are holding much more water.

A single droplet is so small you cannot see it. But you can see a cloud. That's because there are millions and millions and millions of water droplets in a cloud.

Inside the clouds, droplets join together to make drops. The drops get bigger and bigger. When the clouds can no longer hold them, the drops fall to earth.

The sky is full of them. They fall through the air and splatter on the ground.

They are raindrops.

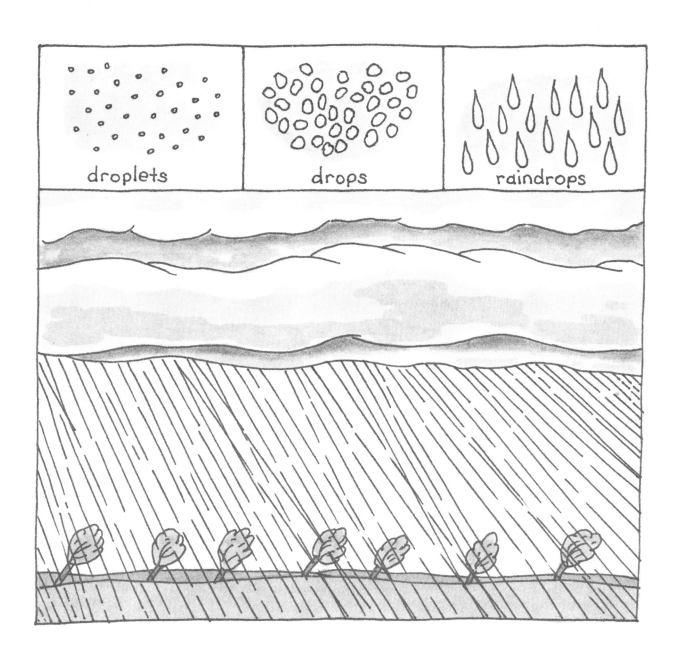

droplets

drops

raindrops

Sometimes the raindrops are small and they fall slowly. It is drizzling.

Sometimes the drops are big and they fall very fast. Now it is pouring.

Sometimes the drops in clouds freeze. These raindrops become ice drops.

This can happen even on a hot day in summer. That's because the clouds and water droplets are carried high above the earth. They may be higher than most airplanes ever go. The higher the clouds, the colder they are. The clouds may be so high, it is freezing cold.

In these high, cold clouds, water vapor changes to droplets, and droplets change to drops. The drops freeze into ice drops. Inside the cloud, these tiny bits of ice start to fall.

But they do not always fall out of the cloud. Instead, they may be carried upward by air that is moving away from the earth.

As they are carried upward, more water collects on the tiny bits of ice. When that water freezes, the drops of ice have another layer on them.

The ice drops are now heavier, so once more they fall toward earth. But air moving away from earth may carry the ice drops upward again. Higher and higher they go, and another layer of ice freezes onto them.

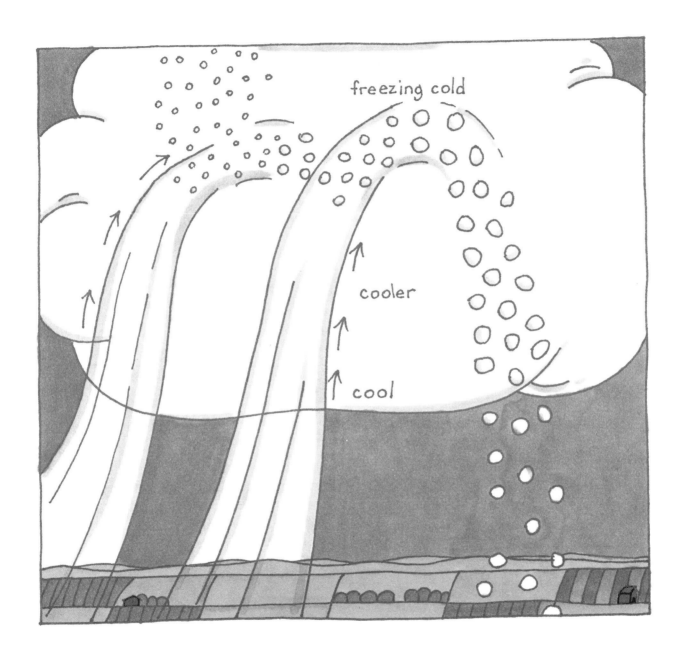

The ice drops get heavier and heavier. They get so heavy that air can no longer carry them upward. So the ice drops fall to earth. It is raining ice.

The ice drops are called hailstones. They may be the size of your fingernail. Or they may be as big as golf balls, or even bigger. In 1970 hailstones as big as softballs fell in Kansas. Fields of corn were flattened by the hailstones.

Hailstones are not stones. They are
pieces of ice.

When it hails, go inside so you're not

cross section
hailstone

hit on the head. When it stops hailing, go
outside again and pick up a hailstone. Break
it in two and you will see the layers of ice.

Water in the clouds makes hail.
Water in the clouds makes rain.
When it stops raining, or hailing, the
sun comes out. Once more, water
evaporates. It evaporates from lakes,
rivers and oceans. Water evaporates from
the leaves of plants and from the wet
ground. It evaporates from cows and
horses, from cats and dogs, and from you
and me.

The water changes to water vapor. It is carried up and away from earth, where the air is cool or even freezing.

When the water vapor cools, it condenses. The water vapor changes to water droplets, and all together the droplets make the clouds.

Water droplets join together to make water drops. The drops fall to earth from the clouds.

Once more it is raining.

About the Author

FRANKLYN M. BRANLEY, Astronomer Emeritus and former
Chairman of The American Museum-Hayden Planetarium, is well
known as the author of many popular books about astronomy
and other sciences for young people of all ages. He is the
originator of the Let's-Read-and-Find-Out Science series.

  Dr. Branley holds degrees from New York University, Columbia
University, and the State University of New York at New Paltz. He
and his wife live in Sag Harbor, New York.

About the Illustrator

HARRIETT WYATT BARTON was born in Picher, Oklahoma, and grew
up in nearby Miami. A graduate of the University of Kansas, she
presently lives in New York City, where she works as Art Director
for a major children's book publisher. She has illustrated a
number of children's books, including *Cactus In The Desert, No
Measles, No Mumps For Me*, and *You Can't Make a Move
Without Your Muscles.*

DATE			
Staff			
staff			